Jasmine's Journey

Jasmine's Journey

Cathy Brown Murphy

Tuckamore Books
a Creative Publishers imprint

St. John's, Newfoundland
2002

Le Conseil des Arts | The Canada Council
du Canada | for the Arts

We acknowledge the support of The Canada Council for the Arts for our
publishing program.

We acknowledge the financial support of the Government of Canada
through the Book Publishing Industry Development Program (BPIDP)
for our publishing program.

Front Cover Art © 2002, Diane Lucas

∞ Printed on acid-free paper

Published by
TUCKAMORE BOOKS
an imprint of CREATIVE BOOK PUBLISHING
a division of 10366 Newfoundland Limited
a Robinson-Blackmore Printing & Publishing associated company
P.O. Box 8660, St. John's, Newfoundland A1B 3T7

First Edition

Printed in Canada by:
ROBINSON-BLACKMORE PRINTING & PUBLISHING

National Library of Canada Cataloguing in Publication Data

Brown Murphy, Cathy, 1957-
        Jasmine's journey / Cathy Brown Murphy.

ISBN 1-894294-49-1

        1. Cats--Juvenile fiction. I. Title.

PS8553.R6934J38   2002   jC813'.6   C2002-902086-7
PZ7

For Jim, who believed in me.

Chapter One

"See you in a little while Jass." The boy pressed his face against the soft cream-coloured flank of the Siamese cat.

"Joel! We have to be at the Wilson's by eight, come on!"

Jasmine laid back her ears. Joel's mom was getting annoyed and her voice was sharp. Joel gave Jasmine one last cuddle and clomped out the door, his big sneakers making the dishes rattle in the cupboard. Watching him leave, Jasmine let her chin drop to her paws and purred blissfully. She adored Joel, her beloved mirow.

Dusk dimmed the corners of the room as the orange sunset gave way to deep blue twilight. Through the window Jasmine could see a single star gleaming high above the spruce trees that sheltered the cottage. The room grew cooler as the dying fire flickered behind the glass doors of the woodstove.

Out of the half-open draught an ember floated, a tiny bright speck. It sailed up and away from the flue. Jasmine watched as the glowing spark settled into the puffy cotton valance that topped the front window. It dimmed for a moment and seemed to die, but suddenly bloomed into a hot tongue of flame. Ears perked forward, the cat watched as the small flame ate into the valance. The smell of burning cloth made her uneasy.

Bits of flaming curtain dropped to the old rag rug below. Soon the rug was smouldering and smoking as the curtain blackened and melted away, gobbled by the hungry flames. Hot embers nibbled greedily at the pine sill behind the curtains.

When the wall above the window was a sheet of flame, Jasmine leapt from her chair. Smoke from the burning rug thickened, the smell of it rank and suffocating. With a muffled whoomph, the rug suddenly exploded into a pool of fire and the flames raced like hot lava, crackling the varnish on the old wooden floor. Jasmine ran to the back corner of the cottage, watching with growing terror as the fire spread with incredible speed.

She scrambled into Joel's bedroom as heavy coils of smoke filled the main room. Breathing was easier here but powerful waves of heat pulsed up from the floor. Jasmine squeezed under the bed, but her favorite hiding place was no refuge now. The hot floor burned her paws and the sizzling air hurt her lungs. Crawling out, she leapt onto the bed. The old quilt, made long ago by Joel's grandmother, was smoking as if it had been laid over hot coals. Though Jasmine couldn't see through the smoke now she felt a tiny breath of fresh air tickle her nose. The fur on her belly was starting to singe as she made a lunge. She found herself on the windowsill. Joel's window was open. Panting, wild-eyed, she threw herself at the open space but bounced off the screen. She dug her claws into the sill to keep from falling to the fiery floor.

She saw there was no escape. Then, from nowhere, a memory of her mother suddenly flashed before her. Squeezing her eyes shut Jasmine saw her, a delicate blue-point Siamese, and heard her urgent voice. "Remember the charm I taught you, the charm that has power when all hope is lost. Let me hear you say it now." Opening her eyes on the inferno surrounding her, Jasmine howled:

"Bastet, Queen of Cats,
Keep me safe between your paws;

When dogs of death snarl at my heels
Snatch me from their jaws!"

Then she threw herself against the screen one more time with all her strength.

The walls of Joel's room were flaming now. By all rights Jasmine's story should end here; such a small cat could never have broken her way through a screen. Maybe it was good luck and rusted staples. But perhaps there really is power in that ancient charm passed down by generations of mother cats to their kittens. The screen gave so abruptly she tumbled out into the grass. She hit the ground and raced into the woods, her mind blanked by panic and terror.

Long minutes passed before she came to herself again. Something seemed wrong. Looking down, she saw the ground far below her. Where am I? she wondered. Her paws gripped so tightly into a tree branch that sap oozed from the bark. Below the branch were many more. Only then did she understand—she was high in a tree. Trembling with shock she settled against the trunk, clinging hard to the branch, to wait out the long night.

Sometime later the distant sound of voices came to her over the roar of the fire as Joel and his family returned to find their cottage a fiery ruin. Not long after she heard a crunching, splintering crash as the timbers collapsed. Then the woods were quiet again.

When the sky finally began to brighten Jasmine was still frozen to her branch. Her scorched paws throbbed painfully. On her belly where the fur had burned off there was a raw patch of skin.

The humans returned as soon as there was light enough for them to see. The cat could hear many people beyond the trees though their words were indistinct. She realized that she was deep in the woods behind where the cottage had been. Then Joel's voice rang out, jarring her out of her state of shock.

"Jass, Jasmine, c'mere girl. It's okay, c'mere Jass." He sounded weary and sad as he walked among the trees calling her name. For the first time in hours she stirred and tried to cry out, but her throat was raw from breathing the hot smokey air; nothing came but a faint, scratchy mew. Long hours of clinging to the branch had cramped her muscles until she couldn't move.

For the rest of the morning she could hear Joel roaming the woods, calling for her. In spite of the pain in her throat Jasmine answered him as best she could but she knew he would never hear her weak cries. Finally, Joel's father appeared. Putting his arms around Joel, he rested his chin on the boy's shaggy brown head. They stood so close to Jasmine's tree, she could hear every word.

"Time to go, Joel. She's gone. There's no way she could have gotten out of that cottage. I'm sorry."

His face wet with tears, Joel pulled away. "You're wrong, she did get out, I know it! Jasmine is smart, she would have found a way to escape." The little cat's heart beat faster, hearing her mirow's words. He knew she was still alive! She opened her mouth to cry out to him but this time no sound came at all.

"Joel, you've called her all morning. We'll ask one of the neighbors to come and check around for Jass every day. There's nothing more we can do. Come on, it's time to head back to Halifax, away from all this." His father took his hand as if he was a very little boy and led Joel away.

Though the fire was long dead, the acrid smell of smoke hung in the air all day. Exhausted, Jasmine slipped in and out of an uneasy sleep. The forest around her gradually came back to life now that the people were gone. Chickadees chased one another from branch to branch. A bluejay screamed from the top of a nearby spruce. A red squirrel eyed Jasmine from the next tree, chittering nervously to himself in a dialect she couldn't understand. All the wild inhabitants were aware of the cat and unsure how much of a threat she might be. Jasmine could smell the rank odour of her fear and knew that it alarmed them.

The heat of the fire and the stress of her wounds had dehydrated her. By the end of the day, thirst began to torment her. As she grew desperate for water Jasmine finally found the will to move again. Very slowly, she unclenched her claws from the tree bark. Her legs were agonizingly stiff. Little by little she stretched herself, shaking from the effort. Then she tried to stand. A nuthatch flew past her with a sharp warning cry, nearly making her lose her precarious balance.

Once on her feet Jasmine realized that climbing back down the tree was impossible. Even if she'd had the strength, the scorched pads of her paws were screaming in protest and her legs trembled like stalks of grass in the wind. With a whimper of misery she lay down again and fell into a fitful sleep.

Scorching flames sprang up around her. With a cry Jasmine flinched as a bright tongue of flame licked at her. Suddenly, a great black cat rose before her, shielding her from the fire.

Jasmine cowered as the cat turned blazing golden eyes upon her.

"Don't be afraid, these flames cannot burn you." Her voice was powerful, but kind. "I am Bastet. I have come to tell you that you have a long journey ahead. It will be perilous, but you must not lose hope. Great love guides your paws; it will take you to your beloved mirow. I promise this."

Everything abruptly went black. With a rasping cry Jasmine woke, feverish and racked with thirst. Such a strange dream. Or was it a dream? she wondered. Bastet's words still rang in her ears. Jasmine closed her eyes, too miserable to think.

The sun was beginning to set. A soft rustling below caught her attention. She looked down to see a chipmunk scrabbling at the base of her tree, burying a pinecone beneath the roots. Jasmine gazed down at his plump, juicy little body with longing. As if he'd read her thoughts, the chipmunk froze, then shot into a crevice beneath the roots.

A wild animal would have been instantly aware of the sudden silence around her. A second ago there had been a riot of territorial cries and whistles. Now, not a single bird called.

The great horned owl struck Jasmine like a

cannonball, careening from the deepening shadows, powerful talons grasping eagerly. But the owl moved like a clumsy youngster just learning to hunt and she miscalculated. Instead of snatching Jasmine off the branch one of her great wings thumped against the cat, knocking Jasmine from her perch. Down she fell, twisting instinctively until her feet were beneath her. She hit the soft forest floor with enough force to jar every bone in her body but took no time to recover; every nerve told her the owl was preparing to strike again. The pain of her burns forgotten, she streaked deep into the woods towards the first refuge she saw, a thick clump of wild raspberry canes. Just as she took cover, the owl passed overhead, her huge yellow eyes searching for her prey. Seeing that the cat had escaped into the thorny tangle she wheeled around and, with an angry hiss, winged away deeper into the forest.

For more than an hour Jasmine lay perfectly still, not daring to move a whisker. A sliver of new moon appeared in the sky. As she watched it rise the cat grew calmer. She was freed from her high perch at last, and water was nearby. She could smell it. Carefully she began to work her way out of the raspberry brambles. Sore and weak, she was glad for the cover of darkness as she picked her way towards the delicious damp smell. The ground grew wet and cool, soothing her blistered paws. Mosquitoes whined around her ears and frogs chirped. Every cell in her body cried out for water as her paws sank in the wet mud of a swamp. She waded into a shallow pool, gratefully lowered her head and began to drink.

After she'd had her fill, Jasmine found a nearby thicket of marsh grass. This dry comfortable bed provided a screen against passing predators so she settled herself and began the long process of licking the soot and mud and blood from her fur.

When morning came she was clean, rested, and no longer thirsty. The burns still throbbed and her body ached but she could feel some strength returning. Lying in the grass she watched as the swamp came alive with birds and insects. A green veil of fresh new growth lay over the forest. Jasmine felt a growing urge to go, but where? She had no desire to return to the ruins of the cottage; the memory of the fire was too terrifying. She wanted Joel. He was out there somewhere. Finding him was the only thing that mattered.

Jasmine raised her head and drifted outside of herself, remembering. Many times she had travelled to the cottage with Joel and his parents, inside the noisy, rattling vehicle that brought them from home. And home was . . . where? A place called Halifax, wherever that might be. That was where Joel was.

Jasmine remembered the dream and Bastet's promise of a long journey that would lead her back to Joel. Was it real? Silently she asked: Bastet, where do I start? In that instant, an interior compass began to turn inside her head. Jasmine felt an urge to turn southward. It felt right. She would begin her journey in that direction.

Fear overwhelmed her for a moment. Halifax was very far away. She knew that from the many long car trips to and from the Amherst Shore cottage. But she pushed her misgivings away. With Bastet's promise and her own keen senses she would find her way to Joel no matter what.

Chapter Two

For the rest of that day Jasmine trotted through the grassy fields and strips of forest that bounded the Northumberland Strait, keeping out of sight of the many cottages she passed. Even though she had been always been raised with love and kindness she knew it was best to avoid strangers. After her escape from the fire and the owl she was beginning to think like a wild animal.

The day was warm and the wind off the water fresh. With her new sense of purpose her pain began to subside but hunger soon replaced it. Two days had passed since her last meal at the cottage, a dish of barbecued salmon. That memory made her empty stomach sqeeze in protest.

Birds flew out of the grass almost under her paws, but she had no idea how to catch one. Her food had always been provided by Joel or his mother. Crossing a meadow fragrant with red clover and purple vetch, she was startled by a grasshopper's sudden spring. It landed on a stalk of timothy a few feet from her, which swayed like a pendulum. Without thinking Jasmine crouched, sized up the distance and pounced. The insect wriggled beneath her paw and she snapped it up. Biting down to stop its frantic squirming she found the body soft and edible but the wings and the spikey legs were impossible; she spat them out.

That night, Jasmine slept restlessly in the branches of a tamarack tree, waking to every rustle and creak as the wind blew through the little grove of trees. Huddled tight against the trunk, she expected every second to feel the claws of an owl tear into her. When dawn finally brightened the eastern sky she was hurting and hungry.

The warm morning wind brought the fresh scent of salt water and mud flats. Keeping on course was easy here; she simply followed the shoreline.

By mid-morning she found a dead Junebug. It looked even less edible than the grasshopper. While poking at it she caught a more appealing scent, one that she'd often picked up in the cottage—mouse. Her chocolate brown ears pricked forward and she crouched, motionless. Just ahead she saw a whorl of dry grass forming the mouth of a small tunnel. From within came the faint rustle of tiny feet. A small grey head appeared at the mouth of the tunnel, bright black eyes cautiously taking in the surroundings. Not even daring to breathe, Jasmine gazed raptly. The mouse scurried a few inches from the nest, whiskers twitching.

She had never caught anything any larger than a moth but it looked simple enough. Get ready, she told herself. One more second . . . now jump! She leapt a heartbeat too soon. The mouse disappeared into his tunnel just as Jasmine landed at the mouth. She dug furiously at the grass though she sensed her prey was gone. Finally she made herself stop and had a calming wash.

Late that afternoon Jasmine came to the banks of the Shinimcas River. The tide was out and the red mudflats gleamed in the sun, cut by a narrow channel of water flowing through the middle. From her vantage point in a nearby field she saw fishing boats leaning against a wooden wharf that jutted from the road which crossed the river. Then the wind veered towards her and she caught a whiff of something irresistible. Her empty belly rolled as she recognized the smell of fish, very ripe fish, rising in nearly-visible waves from the wharf. Seeing no one, she followed her nose to several plastic buckets, one of which was uncovered.

The rancid bait looked like a banquet to the starving cat. She scooped and gobbled the fish as fast as she could, not even stopping when a truck pulled up beside the wharf. A big red-faced man climbed out of the truck.

"Get out of that you!" he boomed. Jasmine dropped the fish tail she was gnawing and ran. Narrowly missing his kick, she streaked down the road and across the Shinimcas. A van swerved around her just before she plunged into the woods.

Between the trees, a sea of tall ferns undulated in the wind. Jasmine picked her way deep into their midst and stretched out. Shaded from the afternoon heat, her belly filled, she drifted into sleep, purring.

The cat woke at dusk and travelled through the night. Perhaps because she was no longer weakened by hunger, she caught her first mouse that night. Nibbling on a wild oat stalk, he didn't even see Jasmine until he was in her jaws. She dispatched him by biting through his neck, growling as fiercely as a lioness on an African veldt. Quivering with excitement and pride she ate every bit but the gall bladder.

The forests and fields along the

Northumberland Strait were alive with activity through the warm summer night. Bats wheeled overhead hunting moths and Junebugs, skunks and racoons dug the soft ground searching for grubs, doe rabbits suckled blind pink babies as they listened for predators; every living thing was hunting or being hunted. Jasmine passed unnoticed among them, not a wild creature but not quite tame now either.

After that night she began to sleep during the afternoons and travel after dark. This nocturnal life suited her feline nature. She felt more awake and alert during the cool evenings and her night vision was excellent. Jasmine's hunting skills continued to improve. Though she was often hungry at least she could find enough nourishment to keep moving.

Four days and nights later Jasmine came to a turning point in her journey. Early in the morning she reached the outskirts of a small town called Pugwash. Here her internal compass told her to turn inland, away from the Northumberland Strait.

Crouching beneath a wild rose bush, hungry and lonely, Jasmine decided to venture a little way into the town to see what she might find. It was easy to cross the broad green lawns and overgrown fields unnoticed. A few dogs hurled threats and curses at her but they were tied and powerless. A garbage can near a shed drew her with a teasing promise of delectable scraps. A quick scan told her no human or animal was near but she found it tightly sealed so she moved on.

She crept into a jungle of a yard behind a dilapidated black shingled house. Lush rugosa rose bushes scattered fuschia-pink petals over the tall grass and the fading mauve blossoms of lilac trees filled the air with the scent of sweet decay. Tangles of honeysuckle vines buzzing with bees spilled over an old wooden fence and up the sides of the house. As she paused to get her bearings, Jasmine heard the low warning growl of another cat. She froze. The pungent smell of tomcat spray suddenly drifted her way. Though it was unfamiliar, instinct told her this cat could be dangerous.

The big orange tom stepped from behind a stack of plant pots on the crooked back step and leapt down beside Jasmine. His fur stood on end, making him look even bigger than he was. Drawing back his upper lip, he bared his fangs and snarled, "This yard is mine!"

Jasmine flattened herself to the ground, trying to look as harmless as possible. He was much too big to fight so she tried to appease him with a humble apology.

"Sorry, I didn't know, I'm new here. I'll leave immediately." She lowered her eyes submissively.

"Too late for that, trespasser!" The orange cat took a step towards her. Arching his back he let out a bone-rattling screech. Just as Jasmine thought the hulking tom was going to tear her to shreds, a quavery voice made him turn and look behind him.

"Marmaduke what do you have there? Oh my, you're the oddest-looking cat I've ever seen. And so thin! You poor little thing. Come here, darling." An old lady in a faded print dress bent and gently ran her hand over Jasmine's shoulder and flank. Looking up, Jasmine yowled a response in her rusty Siamese voice, grateful to be rescued. Marmaduke sat quietly as the woman stroked Jasmine. Slipping her hands under Jasmine's belly she picked her up. Her dress smelled like wood smoke and baking bread. Like all cats, Jasmine could quickly sense loving kindness in another creature. In this mirow it was very strong. Without fear she snuggled against the woman and gave herself over to ecstatic purring, grateful to be safe in someone's arms again.

She was carried inside to a kitchen mostly taken up by a big black wood stove. Setting her down on the cracked linoleum floor, the woman

18

went to the fridge and then to her cupboards, all the while humming to herself. She set a dish of milk before the cat. Jasmine would have turned up her nose at milk before the fire but now she couldn't wait to get at it. The milk was followed by some moist tuna cat food. Forgetting her usual dainty manners Jasmine wolfed it down, not caring about the specks of food on her face and chest. The woman sat nearby watching. "You poor creature; all those scars and scrapes. And when was the last time you had a good feed?"

When Jasmine finished eating she came to sit at the woman's feet.

"You're no ordinary stray, I can see that. I believe you're one of those fancy Siamese cats I've seen pictures of." She picked Jasmine up and settled her in her lap. The tired cat fell asleep then and there without even washing.

Jasmine woke to find herself on a sofa in a room off the kitchen. It was early evening and the room was filled with shadows. The sofa was dusted with cat hairs and the scent of other cats was everywhere though none were visible. A faint smell of roses drifted from a glass bowl of faded potpourri on the fireplace mantle. Scanning the darkening room she saw a hard-looking upholstered chair and a dusty glass-fronted cabinet containing several birds. Jasmine's ears and whiskers went up in astonishment. Never before had she seen birds in a house. And why were they sitting so quietly? she wondered. Testing the air with her nose, she found they were nothing but dried-out skins and feathers with the pulse of life long gone from them. Why would anyone want such horrible things? she wondered, looking at them unesasily.

A sudden movement caught her eye, and she was startled to see a child standing by the fireplace. Strangely, no scent came from him, no sweet, musty boy-smell like Joel's. This child was several years younger than Joel and dressed in short pants and a white shirt with black boots on his feet. He took no notice of anything else in the room, not even Jasmine, as he reached up to touch the bowl of potpourri on the mantle. Then, to the cat's astonishment, he began to fade. His dimming figure fell into glittering fragments that melted away on the brick hearth like ice crystals on a stove.

"Don't worry, that's only little Hughie. He's always hanging around the fireplace. He's quite harmless."

Jasmine peeked cautiously over the edge of the sofa and saw a plump grey-striped cat looking up at her.

"My name's Montague by the way. You'll

soon get used to the house spirits if you stay here. They're actually pretty boring for the most part. They don't even notice us."

"Oh . . . really? Well uh, hullo. My name's Jasmine. How many cats live here anyway?"

"Six of us right now. It's too bad you met that old Marmaduke first. We heard him yowling at you in the yard this morning. He's not very bright so he makes up for it by being a bully; fortunately he spends most of his time outside since he has the unpleasant habit of spraying everything to mark it as his."

"Where are the others?"

"In the kitchen with Mamacat. I came to see if you were awake so you could meet them. Follow me."

Jasmine jumped from the sofa and padded along behind Montague, happy to leave the room. She doubted she would get used to the 'house spirits.'

In the kitchen, the old woman sat in a bentwood rocker so big her feet barely touched the floor. In her hand was a glass filled with a golden drink that smelled to Jasmine like strawberries and vinegar mixed together. Four cats sat on various perches around the kitchen drowsing or washing. Jasmine suddenly remembered the flecks of food on her face and felt shy. Montague settled near the woman's chair, tucking his tail carefully around his feet well out of the way of the big rockers.

"That's Millicent there under the table." He nodded toward a grey cat with a white chin and paws who blinked at them and ducked her head timidly. "Merlyn is under the stove," Montague continued, glancing at a handsome black cat with long hair. "Minerva and Matilda are on the table, though Mamacat doesn't like us to sit there. They're sisters. It's almost impossible to tell them apart." The two white cats, each with one blue eye and one golden, regarded Jasmine with frank curiousity.

"We haven't seen a cat like you before," one of the sisters said. Jasmine gave herself a couple of self-conscious licks.

"I am Siamese. Please excuse my appearance. I've been on a long journey and I haven't had time to tidy myself. Who is this Mamacat you've been talking about?" All the cats stared at her, round-eyed with amazement.

"Well her of course, the mirow who looks after us all," Montague said, glancing up at the woman. "She is no ordinary mirow. We were all abandoned, homeless cats; Mamacat rescued us. We owe our lives to her. She's been a mother to us and more."

"I sensed that she was special as soon as we met," Jasmine said.

One by one the other cats went back to washing or napping. Grateful she was no longer the centre of attention, Jasmine began to clean her fur as well. As the evening passed, Mamacat rocked and sipped her strange smelling brew with her little family of felines around her. The cats continued to speak amongst themselves, mind to mind and heart to heart. Jasmine wondered what Mamacat would think if she knew her cats were talking. It had always seemed strange to her that mirows could be so oblivious to what the cats around them were saying. Even the most beloved mirows, like Joel.

When Mamacat began to sing to herself in a wavering voice Montague told Jasmine, "We'll be turning in for the night soon. We always do after she starts singing." Sure enough, Mamacat got to her feet somewhat unsteadily and turned off the lights. The cats all watched as she made her way, still singing, across the room, then they followed her up the stairs in an orderly procession. Mamacat held tight to the railing as she slowly climbed. Jasmine wondered why she suddenly seemed so off balance and full of song. Was it because of that rusty-looking liquid she'd been sipping all evening?

By the time Mamacat was ready to sleep, all five cats had arranged themselves on her big double bed; Montague on one of the pillows, Merlyn halfway down. At the foot of the bed Millicent stretched out on one side and Minerva and Matilda curled up together on the other. Mamacat squeezed herself under the covers with a drowsy goodnight to them all. No one invited Jasmine to join them. Since there was no room on the bed anyway, she leapt lightly to the top of the dresser and curled up among the perfume bottles and brushes and talc cans. From there she watched the moon, almost full now, make its course across the night sky until sleep came.

At the darkest time of the night, between moonset and sunrise, Jasmine suddenly woke, every sense on full alert. Something was wrong. A chill lay over her like an icy blanket. Looking up she saw a very old man bending over her. Every hair stood on end and she bared her fangs in a silent snarl as he leaned closer. Like Hughie, he had no scent. He wore a long black coat and his empty eyes looked right through her. His boney hands reached towards her and Jasmine knew she would screech in terror if he touched her. She longed to sink her claws into his grey face but there was no flesh there to tear into. He had no more substance than the boy beside the fireplace. She snarled again, a low growl bubbling up in her throat, and at last he backed away. Parting his lips he blew out an icy breath and she saw his teeth were black stumps. Then he dissolved and fell away to a few dwindling sparkles like dying fireworks.

Jasmine spent the rest of the night wide-awake and watchful while the others slept undisturbed. Why had this hideous spirit come to her? Hadn't Montague told her that the ghosts never bothered with the cats? Shivering, Jasmine listened to the woman's rhythmic snores and wondered how anyone could sleep peacefully in such a place. She didn't dare to close her eyes again until the morning sun came streaming through the window.

It felt as if she had just gotten to sleep when Mamacat began to stir. The old woman freed her legs from Merlyn's weight, sat up, and pushed her feet into slippers. The cats on the bed woke as well, stretching and yawning. Matilda began washing Minerva's ears.

Jasmine barely had her eyes open when Mamacat, her white hair bristling like straw, came to the bureau, reaching for her brush.

"What have you got there, little one?" she asked. To Jasmine's surprise she took a small black and white photograph from beneath the cat's paw. It hadn't been there the night before, Jasmine was sure. Mamacat gave a sharp gasp. "Where in the world did this come from?" Her lined old face suddenly seemed to collapse and her blue eyes filmed with tears. "It's little Hughie—I thought this picture was lost forever. We turned the house upside down looking for it after he died. How did it end up here after all this time?" The woman's voice broke as she pulled on her robe and hurried from the room, still peering at the photograph. All the cats followed her except for little Millicent.

"What happened? Where did that picture come from? I'm sure it wasn't here last night," Jasmine fretted.

"Sometimes, the spirits bring her things. She doesn't always notice if it's just junk like buttons or bits of glass, but sometimes they bring her things she wants, like that old piece of paper. I think they do it to let her know they're here but it doesn't make any difference. She never seems to see them."

"How can she miss them? They're everywhere. Last night there was a horrible ghost right in this room! He must have brought that picture." Jasmine shuddered. "Why do we see the spirits when the mirows don't?"

"We cats see, hear and smell plenty of things that mirows don't. You must have noticed that. I've thought a lot about these ghosts. I think they're like shadows that get left behind when the mirows die and go to Summerland. It's different for us cats. We go through so many reincarnations before Bastet finally takes us to Summerland. I don't think there's enough left after we die to leave behind a shadow. We come right back again, as kittens."

"They do seem more like shadows than living things. There isn't much to them. Who is Hughie? He must have been important to Mamacat."

"Hughie was her little brother. She talks to us about him a lot. He died a long time ago but she still misses him."

"I think I saw him last night by the fireplace. This is a strange place. Do you like living here?"

The little grey cat gave herself a couple of self-conscious licks then looked at Jasmine, her big green eyes bright with emotion.

"It doesn't matter where I live as long as I'm with Mamacat; I love her. She saved my life."

"I know what it's like to love a mirow like that. I'd like to hear your story if you don't mind," Jasmine said shyly.

Millicent bowed her head for a moment and

then began. "I was born in a garage. My mother made the best nest she could for me and my two brothers on a pile of old rags but I remember how cold it was. We were born too early; it must have been barely spring. Still, it wasn't all bad. Mother spent most of her time snuggling us and filling our bellies with her warm milk. But that all ended the day our eyes opened. The world was still very blurry but I will never be able to forget the terrible mirow who came into the garage that day. My mother knew him; she growled and snarled but he just pushed her away. He grabbed me and my brothers and shoved us into an old burlap bag. After that there was darkness. We were tossed about roughly and we clung to each other, crying in terror. The next thing I remember, the bag was filling with cold water. But one corner of it didn't sink. We clung to that little space for a long time, trying to stay above the freezing water.

"That cold water felt like all I'd ever known. My voice was tiny but I cried out with all my might. And by some miracle Mamacat heard me. She found that sack in a water-filled ditch not far from here and she pulled it out. When she opened it my brothers were cold and still and I was barely alive. Mamacat brought me here and warmed me and fed me. I've been here ever since." Millicent shivered as she came to the end of her tale.

Overcome with pity and horror Jasmine jumped to the bed and began to comfort Millicent the only way she could, by gently washing her as if she were a small kitten. Wishing she could somehow wash away the little cat's suffering, Jasmine groomed her until Millicent slipped into the peace of sleep.

For two more days Jasmine stayed with Mamacat and her family. There were no more encounters with house spirits. Most of her time was spent with Millicent. They ate from the same dish and spent long hours talking. When they sat together they crossed tails, as cats do when they are best friends. Jasmine found comfort in telling about her own misfortunes.

Jasmine knew she was welcome to stay as long as she liked but she was eager to be on her way again as she regained her strength. A long journey lay ahead and each day she stayed was another day away from Joel. On the night of the full moon she decided it was time. A window over the kitchen sink was always left open a few inches so the indoor cats could come and go. Jasmine waited until the woman and the cats made their nightly trip up the stairs to bed, Mamacat weaving and humming happily up the stairs. Millicent stayed behind in the darkened kitchen watching Jasmine.

"You're leaving, aren't you." It was a statement, not a question.

"Yes, how did you know?"

"That's what I'd be doing if I were separated from my mirow," Millicent replied.

"I'm glad you understand. I'm grateful for the chance to stop here and rest, but I have to go back to searching for my boy Joel. Nothing else matters," Jasmine told her.

"Be careful Jasmine. You know what Marmaduke tells us? Never trust a mirow. He says any of them will dispose of us as soon as we are trouble, except Mamacat. Marmaduke is crazy, but there's some truth in what he says; I ought to know. We both have mirows we love, but there are plenty of bad ones out there and even more that are stupid or uncaring."

"I'll be careful. Goodbye, Millicent. You will always be in my thoughts." She touched her nose to Millicent's. "May Bastet hold you between her paws," she murmured, bestowing the ancient blessing of cats.

"And you also," Millicent replied.

Then with a graceful leap Jasmine was up and through the open window.

It was a glorious summer night. Far off along

the shore fireworks were cracking and blazing. Jasmine paused a moment, remembering other summer nights like this. The noise and the explosions of the fireworks had always frightened her until she was snuggled safely in Joel's arms. But then, she would let him carry her down to the beach and they would watch the displays together.

It was time to move. With her back to the Northumberland Strait and her nose to the far-off Atlantic Ocean, she set off south, a shadow passing in the night.

Chapter Three

By morning the grassy meadows and open spaces were swallowed by dense forest, with no roads or human habitation. Rested and well-fed, Jasmine made good progress in the next few days. Mice were plentiful that summer. On the second day she came upon the half-eaten carcass of a grouse near an alder-choked stream. On full alert in case the predator that had killed the bird returned, she nibbled the scraps of meat remaining on the bones.

Jasmine was finished and washing her face and whiskers when a musky, familiar smell wafted her way. She'd often picked it up while travelling through fields, though she hadn't yet seen the creature that created it. Hearing a rustle among the alders, she scrambled swiftly up a nearby poplar. As soon as she was out of sight, a scrawny fox kit stumbled out of the bushes and fell on the bones of the bird, tearing at them ravenously. From above the cat saw the little creature was no threat to her. He was even smaller than she was, barely weaned and surely too young to be on his own. She waited until she was sure the cub was alone. Then curiousity got the better of her and she climbed down for a closer look.

The little fox stopped eating long enough to take a quick glance at her, then went back to chewing the bones and gristle.

"This is mine. Go away!" he yipped.

"Take it. I've had enough." Jasmine sat nearby and watched him eat though she knew she should be moving on. The kit was no concern of hers and she needed to find a safe place to sleep away the afternoon.

When every edible scrap was devoured the fox flopped down with his chin between his paws, a picture of dejection. The cat's inquisitive nature got the better of her.

"What are you?" she asked. The kit raised his little black snout. His eyes were golden like a cat's.

"I'm a fox. What are you?"

"Where is your mother?" she asked, ignoring his question.

"She went away to hunt and never came back. Me and my sisters got hungrier and hungrier, so

I left the den to look for her and I got lost." His chin dropped back between his paws.

Jasmine wondered what to do. She was barely surviving herself, and there were so many miles ahead of her. Why should I care what happens to him? she asked herself. We're all on our own here, like it or not. Turning abruptly, she left him beside the scattered bones and slipped out of the little clearing. But before she got very far she turned to find the little fox following her. Vexed, she dodged through brush trying to lose him. But when she finally stopped to catch her breath, she saw him peeking out at her from behind a clump of ferns.

"Go away! I can't help you!" she growled. The cub sat down, raised his little muzzle and let out a mournful wail.

"Hush you foolish thing! Keep howling like that and every predator for miles will come after us."

"I want my mother," he whimpered. His red fur was matted and dirty and he was trembling. Looking at him made Jasmine remember her first time away from her mother. She'd been so miserable that first night, all alone in the cardboard box that was supposed to be her bed. Where were the warm bodies of her brothers and sisters, the gentle rasp of her mother's tongue?

Sometime during the night, Joel had heard her squalling and went to her. Scooping her out of the box he brought her to his bed and cuddled her until she'd fallen to sleep. Until the fire, she'd spent every night of her life after that sleeping beside him, warm and content. What if Joel had just left her to cry her heart out?

Jasmine gave the fox cub a lick between his ears. It was going to take hours to clean him, but she'd decided. She couldn't leave him here to die. She was lonely and he would be company for her. Besides, he was a wild thing and would surely learn to survive quickly. Maybe they could help each other.

"C'mon, we have to find a place to rest. By the way my name is Jasmine. I'm a cat," she told him.

The little fox scrambled to his feet eagerly. "I don't have a name."

"Then I'll call you Yip. It suits you."

She led him to a crevice between two large granite boulders she'd spotted earlier. They squeezed in and found dry ground padded with a thick layer of dead leaves. It was as safe a refuge as could be hoped for. Jasmine laid down and the cub curled up beside her, laying his head on her shoulder. Cleaning and smoothing his fur, she noticed she was already getting used to his musky smell.

"I'm glad you found me," he murmured when she had finished with him. Instantly he fell into an exhausted sleep. Jasmine, however, did not. Beside him in their cozy nest she wondered how she was going to cope with this new responsibility.

They stayed near the crevice another night and day while Jasmine did her best to provide for them. Yip watched enthralled as she caught a fat mouse hidden beneath a small pile of brush.

"How did you know it was there?" he asked. Jasmine brought the dead mouse to Yip and laid it at his feet.

"Smell it," she urged. Yip lowered his pointed nose and sniffed the mouse.

"Smells good." He licked his lips.

"You'll remember that smell now. And that's how you find mice; they always hide, so you have to find them with your nose."

"Can we eat it now?" Yip begged.

"Sure. You can take the first bite," Jasmine told him, feeling proud. Against all odds, she was becoming a competent hunter and a provider. Surely Bastet was watching over her.

She was relieved to find Yip a quick learner. By the second day he was catching grasshoppers on his own. That afternoon the cat found a pheasant's nest hidden in a clump of blueberry bushes and they feasted on the clutch of eggs. The kit quickly regained his spirit and energy and Jasmine decided it was time to move on. Yip would have to learn as they went.

All that afternoon thunder rumbled beyond the Wentworth hills. Jasmine and Yip left the clearing early in the evening just as the first drops of rain pattered down. As much as she hated being wet, she kept going. She knew she could endure a warm summer rain.

Travelling on through the woods, they passed close to several hunting and vacation camps. Most seemed empty but Jasmine took care to stay well away from them. As it grew dark she slowed, but Yip had no problem adjusting to her nocturnal schedule. His night vision was at least as good as hers. Perhaps because he was so young he was proving to be more adaptable than she had expected.

They stopped to rest and hunt late the next morning. Unfortunately they had come to a sparse, rocky area that held nothing edible, just scrub and wild blueberry bushes. The cat and the kit bedded down, tired and hungry, beneath the branches of a fallen spruce tree.

"We'll find food tomorrow," she assured him.

Yip nuzzled against her for comfort. "Tomorrow . . ." he murmured, his eyes closing as weariness overcame his hunger.

When Jasmine woke early that evening the kit was already up and sniffing around. "Jasmine, I smell something good." He ran off a little then stopped. "Aren't you coming?"

"Wait! You have to learn to wait—never rush into anything," she scolded. "There's danger everywhere. If you get too excited and you think you might do something foolish, just stop and give your face a good wash. It calms you right down and gives you time to think." The little fox sat and began clumsily rubbing a paw over his black muzzle like a cat while Jasmine tested the air. She knew immediantly what had caught Yip's attention. It was the aroma of meat grilling on a barbecue. Her mouth watered as she remembered the tidbits of barbecued steak and chicken she had eaten at the cottage. Almost against their will, the two began to creep towards temptation. They didn't have to go far. In a hollow just below them was a tin-roofed vacation shack. An unattended barbecue sat on the crooked deck, sending up plumes of rich, greasy smoke. Jasmine felt as if a raging demon had been unleashed in her belly.

"You wait here. I'll go for a closer look. If you

see anyone, run!" Jasmine commanded. Yip crouched obediently behind the stump where they had stopped. Leaving the protection of the woods, Jasmine inched her way towards the deck, closer and closer. No sign or scent of dog, she was relieved to notice. Now she could hear the fat from the steaks sizzling as it dripped into the hot coals. The humans were inside the cabin. She could hear the murmur of their voices. She crept onto the deck, then across to the barbecue. Leaping onto the wooden shelf attached to the grill, she sized up the meat, now just inches from her nose. Wondering how she would manage to snatch a steak off the hot spitting grill, she didn't see the man come up behind her until it was too late.

Jasmine was gripped gently but firmly by a large bearded man. Because she had been raised in a loving home it didn't occur to her to bite him, but she did squirm and kick frantically.

"It's okay puss. I won't hurt you. Maureen, come and see what I've got here!" he called. As Jasmine tried to thrash her way out of his grip, a woman with long red hair and faded blue overalls came out of the cabin.

"A Siamese cat! Where could that have come from? We're miles from the nearest house!" she exclaimed. Cautiously she reached out to touch

Jasmine's chocolate-brown ear. "Just look at those blue eyes," she said admiringly. Jasmine was beginning to relax a little when a familiar yipping grabbed her attention. The small red fox came hurtling out of the woods towards the deck, barking at the humans in the fiercest voice he could manage.

"Yip, you fool, get out of here!" Jasmine howled. He skidded to a halt, suddenly unsure of himself. The two people stared at him, mouths agape. Distracted, the man loosened his hold on the cat. With a powerful twist she freed herself and the two animals went streaking back into the forest, leaving a pair of startled humans behind them.

They ran until they were exhausted, until the cabin was far behind. Panting, they finally dropped onto a bed of ferns. After a moment Yip raised his head, his jaws split in a wide fox's grin. "Did you see the look on their faces?"

Jasmine responded by laying back her ears. With a sudden leap she knocked him on his back and began to chew his ears, though gently. "You're crazy, taking a chance like that! What am I going to do with you!" They wrestled in the ferns, nipping playfully at one another, rolling over and over. Jasmine discovered that Yip had grown in the few days they had been together; he was as big as she was now and quite capable of pinning her to the ground.

When they finished playing, Jasmine said, "I want you to listen to me now, this is important. The first thing your mother would have taught you is to always stay away from mirows." They were laying down among the ferns, panting. "Don't ever let them see you if you can help it. You are a wild animal. You can never trust them."

Crawling on his belly, Yip inched his way to her side and licked her nose. "I'm sorry Jasmine. When that big mirow grabbed you I got so scared I didn't stop to think."

Closing her eyes Jasmine nestled against her friend. "You're still just a kit after all. Thank you for rescuing me."

"I wish we could have grabbed that meat though—I'm so hungry," Yip sighed.

"I think we'll stay here for tonight. I don't know know about you but I don't have the energy to travel. Maybe tomorrow will bring better luck," Jasmine told him. They settled into a dense clump of ferns and immediately fell asleep in spite of their empty bellies.

They woke early the next morning, ravenously hungry. While testing the air Jasmine's attention was caught by a rustle just beyond their clump of ferns. Peering out she saw a young buck rabbit nibbling the tender new tips of nearby fir branches. Jasmine froze, instantly alert, and Yip copied her. She pressed the fox down with her paw, signalling that he was to stay put, then she slipped off towards her prey. Intoxicated by the fresh green branches, the rabbit was oblivious as Jasmine crept closer and closer.

Flattening herself to the ground Jasmine measured the distance between them, every nerve in her lithe body twitching. Then she sprang. Just as she'd hoped, the rabbit bolted in Yip's direction. An instant later a shrill scream told her that Yip had managed to bring the rabbit down. Racing over to them she saw that Yip had fixed his sharp teeth into the neck of his prey but hadn't succeeded in killing it. Jasmine leapt onto the panicking creature before it could escape, biting deep into the soft throat. The rabbit kicked once, then relaxed into death.

The cat and the fox feasted until they could eat no more, then went on their way, leaving the bones for the ravens to pick.

As they trotted along through the hot, still woods Jasmine worried that their progress was too slow. Since her near capture the night before she had become anxious to leave Wentworth behind. They kept moving when the cool of evening came, not stopping to rest until the first flush of dawn. The weather was good and the hunting improved. They covered so much ground, by the next morning Jasmine and Yip found themselves on the edge of a grassy plain, the salty tang of the Minas basin in their noses.

The forest thinned and miles of pasture and saltmarsh stretched before them. When they had their first glimpse of the open space, Yip was astonished; all his brief life he had been wrapped in the leafy arms of the woods.

"There's nothing above us here! How will we keep from being seen?"

Jasmine was amused by his reaction. "We'll be fine, Yip. The grass is tall; it'll hide us." She knew that they were at greater risk of being seen from above by owls and hawks but decided not to alarm Yip any more for now.

They soon discovered that the grassland was home to armies of field mice. Hunting had never been easier and during the next few days the fox cub became proficient at catching them. Watching him trotting over to her with a fat mouse dangling from his jaws, Jasmine felt relief mixed with sorrow. Yip could now provide for himself. Soon she could leave him.

"This would be a good area to settle down in," she told the kit.

"But you're going to find your mirow. We can't stay here," Yip said.

But you can't come with me, little fox, don't you know that? Jasmine thought sadly. Yip trotted over to her with the mouse and dropped it at her feet. She felt a rush of maternal pride. She had taught him well.

"Eat it," she said, nosing it towards him. "That's your mouse. You caught it."

It would soon be time to face reality. She couldn't lead the fox into danger. Jasmine had become very fond of him but she had known from the first that she couldn't bring Yip with her to Joel, who lived in an area teeming with mirows. That was no place for a wild animal. It was time to start looking for a place where Yip could stay behind. Her heart sank at the thought of travelling on without her little companion.

Still heading south, Jasmine and Yip soon found their way blocked by Cobequid Bay. After they skirted Masstown they came to a wide stretch of mudflats spreading as far as they could see. Hiding in the tall marsh grass they studied the bay, their noses working busily as they took in all the rich smells of the shoreline.

"We can't cross here, that's for sure. Look how fast that water is moving over the mud," Jasmine said.

Yip stared, amazed. "I didn't know there was that much water in the world."

"I guess we'll have to go around this somehow," the cat said after they had watched the swiftly moving tide for a few more minutes. They had gone only a half-mile through the marsh grass when Yip suddenly halted.

"Smell that? There are foxes here," he told Jasmine.

Breathing deeply, she caught a faint whiff of the musky scent that was now so familar to her. "Let's see where it's coming from," she suggested. Yip followed obediently as they trotted along through the sweet-smelling grass. Soon they came to a a rocky outcrop rising above the salt-marsh topped by a ragged clump of black spruce. A sharp foxy scent drifted down to them.

"That's where their den is, in those rocks," Yip told her.

"Let's stop here a while and see if we can get a look at them," she said, her heart heavy at the thought of what she had to do.

"What if they're not friendly?"

"We'll hide over there in the tall grass. They won't even know we're here," Jasmine said, hoping to reassure him. She didn't feel safe near the foxes' den but it was a chance she had to take, for Yip's sake. He'd have a better chance of survival if he could stay with his own kind, she was certain. He was still so young. He had much to learn.

The sun slid down until it seemed to rest on the edge of the grassland, casting a brilliant blaze of orange and salmon above the horizon. Jasmine kept watch, her bright eyes gleaming. A fresh wind off the bay stirred the tall grass that screened them. Yip was napping when the foxes finally left their den. Just as the sun disappeared, Jasmine saw a female and three half-grown cubs, not much older than Yip. Raising her sharp black muzzle, the vixen tested the air, but the wind was in Jasmine's favour. The mother led her cubs off to the marsh without detecting the trespassers.

The cat watched Yip sleep, knowing that she was going to miss him unbearably. He was such a playful, bright companion. Taking care of him had taken her mind off her own sorrow. And helping him to become independent had given Jasmine new confidence in herself. She and Yip were both going to be survivors; she was sure of it. This would be a good place for him. There was plenty of prey and no sign of mirows. She hoped that the other foxes would accept him into their clan but if they didn't, there was still lots of space for him.

It would be easiest to just slip away but if she

did, she knew he would simply follow her scent. Somehow she had to convince him to stay behind.

She licked his muzzle and ears to wake him. Yip stretched, cat-like, relishing the attention.

"I've got something important to say, Yip." Jasmine gave one of his black-tipped ears a gentle nip to get his attention. "I want you to stay here with the other foxes."

He scrambled to his feet instantly. "What do you mean stay here—I'm coming with you!"

"You can't. You know I'm going far away to find Joel. He lives in a place with many other mirows. You wouldn't be safe there. We both knew that all along, and now we have to face it. I want you to stay here. This is a good place for you. It feels safe and there's other foxes around. If you try to follow me I'll have to run away from you. Please don't make me do that."

Yip lay down, dropping his muzzle on his front paws, just as he had the first time they met. But this time Jasmine hardened her heart. She bent her head and nuzzled him.

"Look how big you've grown. You're a good hunter now too. I know you'll be okay, Yip. I don't want to leave you but I have no choice."

"Please don't go," he whimpered.

Cats don't cry as humans do but Jasmine felt a painful tightness in her chest.

"This is best. You'll understand some day when you have kits of your own. If you miss me just remember, I'll be missing you twice as much." She pressed her chocolate-brown nose against his, then turned and slipped away as fast as she could without running. One long wail reached her through the darkness. It stopped her in her tracks, but only for a moment. Nearly choking on her sorrow, she sped away from Yip.

The next three days and nights passed in a blur of misery as the saltmarshes gave way to pasture. Outside the town of Truro there were sprawling fields and farmhouses. The huge silhouettes of cattle alarmed Jasmine until she saw that they took no notice of her; still she kept her distance from them.

Trotting along the edge of a woodlot early in the morning, she sensed that she was being followed. Pausing beside a twisted tamarack she tried the air for a scent, hoping with all her heart that Yip had not followed her after all. A dog-like odour suddenly came to her on the cool early-morning air. An instant later she was running for her life.

Though she had never encountered a coyote before she knew instinctively this was a deadly enemy. Streaking across the pasture she had no time to plan her course. The coyote was already close behind. Jasmine caught a quick glimpse of the animal pursuing her; a young female so scrawny that her grey-brown hide hung on her bones like an old rug.

The cat's paws barely touched the ground, but the long legged coyote gained steadily. Jasmine barely had time to notice a barbed wire fence before she had passed under the bottom wire. It took the larger coyote an instant longer to crawl beneath but she was quickly on Jasmine's tail again, her tongue hanging out as she loped easily along. Soon she was so close Jasmine could hear her panting. Desperately, she veered to the left, leaving her pursuer scrambling to change direction. At the edge of the pasture, looming just ahead, was a row of houses. The cat raced towards a weathered old garage behind the nearest. There was no time to think; she could only trust her instincts. Jasmine leapt up and through the window of the garage before she knew it was open. Like a bird, she sailed through the missing bottom pane and hit the dusty floor on all four paws.

The chase had captured the attention of the neighborhood dogs. They began to raise a great din, barking and howling hysterically. Panting, the coyote paused beneath the window. Jasmine crouched inside, waiting to see what her pursuer would do next. Could she squeeze through the window? Would she dare to try? Few wild creatures would willingly enter such an enclosed space, so close to human habitation. This was her only hope. Ears straining, she listened. Over the howling of the dogs she heard the coyote's angry snarl. Long minutes passed. Finally, the dogs quieted and Jasmine knew the coyote was gone.

For the rest of the day she cowered in the garage, perched on a stack of old lumber piled to the ceiling. Dust tickled her nose as she huddled there trembling, too terrified to move. As the day wore on, the beam of light spilling through the window made its way across the dirty wooden floor and she gradually calmed. Children's voices drifted past with other summertime neighborhood sounds; squeaky clotheslines, purring lawn mowers, whispering lawn sprinklers.

As the shock of her near-fatal encounter with the coyote wore off Jasmine felt utterly exhausted. The last few weeks suddenly seemed more than she could bear—the terrifying fire, the long miles, the constant hunger, the heartbreaking decision to leave Yip behind. For the first time Jasmine wondered if she would ever see Joel again. Like a rebuke, the memory of Bastet's promise came back to her. She bowed her head. "I'm sorry, Queen Bastet," she said, "I didn't know it would be so hard. I just can't go any further." Crouched in the hot, stuffy garage Jasmine finally gave up.

When the big doors creaked open late in the afternoon she waited without hope, too weary to run from whatever came next.

What came next was a little girl with toffee-coloured braids wearing a bathing-suit and shorts. As the doors swung open, a sunbeam fell on Jasmine like a spotlight. The girl had started to reach for the hose on the wall when she saw the little cream-coloured cat. She stared, entranced.

"Where did you come from?" she asked, keeping her voice soft so it wouldn't startle the cat. Jasmine replied with a deep Siamese yowl that caused the girl's eyes to widen.

"You have a big voice for such a little cat," she breathed. "Don't move, I'll be right back." She turned and ran out of the garage. In a couple of minutes she returned with a package of sliced ham and a bowl slopping over with water. She set them down on a dusty work bench, then backed away and squatted by the garage doors. The smell of food and water was irresistible. There seemed nothing left to lose, so Jasmine jumped from the lumber pile to the bench and extracted a slice of ham from the package, devouring it in seconds. Her long hours in the hot garage had left her so thirsty that she lapped the water eagerly. Dipping her nose too deep, she sneezed violently like a kitten just learning to drink from a bowl.

The little girl watched without a word. Jasmine had almost forgotten she was there by the time the meal was finished. As Jasmine began to wash her face, the girl stood and walked slowly towards her. Cautiously, she reached a hand towards the cat and gently stroked her, all the while speaking in a low crooning murmur. Tensing, Jasmine considered her options; run past the girl and through the open door or stay and see what would happen next? As the minutes passed, Jasmine began to relax. The child's touch was comforting. It would feel so good to be taken care of for a while; she was tired of struggling to survive each day. When the girl gathered her up in her arms, Jasmine didn't protest.

She was carried through the back door and into the kitchen.

"Mom, look what I found in the garage!" the girl called to the woman standing in front of the stove. "She was hiding in there. Look how thin she is. I can feel every bone in her body."

"The poor little thing. Purebred cats like this usually aren't strays, Elizabeth. She must belong to someone. Maybe she's lost."

"We'd better keep her then, until we find her owners," Elizabeth said quickly.

"I hope she doesn't have fleas," Elizabeth's mother sighed. "Don't get too attached. Somebody will be wanting her back. And remember, you're the one who'll take care of the cat, not me!"

Jasmine spent that night curled up on Elizabeth's bed, having been inspected by her mother and found to be free of fleas. Before bedtime, she was given all the food she could eat, and Elizabeth had brushed her coat until it gleamed. Jasmine felt relieved to be safe under the roof of mirows again. Elizabeth seemed to be a kind, gentle girl. Lying on clean, soft sheets Jasmine thought, I could just stay here. It would be such an easy life. This would be a good home for any cat.

She had slept in the wild for so long that every little sound that first night startled her into heart-pounding alertness. Never again would she sleep soundly.

When she woke in the morning she leapt lightly to the floor. Elizabeth's brown eyes opened as soon as the cat left the bed. She grinned, showing two spaces where her baby teeth had fallen out.

"Wait for me!" She climbed out of bed and picked up the cat and Jasmine snuggled against her, breathing in the fresh smell of cotton pajamas dried in the sun and wind.

They went down the stairs to the kitchen.

"Your dad picked up some cat chow before he went to work. Pour some into that dish on the counter and make sure she has fresh water," Elizabeth's mom called from the deck where she was drinking coffee. Elizabeth put Jasmine down and followed her mother's instructions, then got herself some juice and a granola bar.

The rest of the day passed peacefully. Jasmine dozed on an old blanket Elizabeth's mother had placed on an easy chair in the den. Her naps were broken by frequent processions of neighborhood children Elizabeth led to have a look at the exotic cat she had found. Elizabeth's mother let Jasmine out in the afternoon and she discovered a sandy place under the deck that would do for her litter box. But as soon as she was done she hurried to the door and yowled to be let inside again. To be outside now felt terrifying, as if potential predators were lurking in every shadow. When the woman let her in she was glad to return to her blanket.

Two weeks passed. Jasmine was well cared for in Elizabeth's house. But in spite of that, she felt sad and anxious. The choice morsels of food that filled her bowl seemed tasteless. The toys Elizabeth brought her went untouched. She soon grew tired of the girl's attention. She wanted to growl whenever Elizabeth picked her up for a cuddle and then she felt ashamed. Joel never was far from her thoughts and she fretted as the summer days passed.

Every time she ventured outside panic overwhelmed her. The coyote was long gone but she had left permanent scars on Jasmine's heart.

Elizabeth began to lose interest in the cat. Jasmine showed her little affection. One day, watching as Jasmine squirmed out of Elizabeth's arms yet again her mother shook her head. "That cat isn't very cuddly, is she?"

Elizabeth frowned. "I don't think she likes me at all, Mom."

"Be patient. We don't know what she went through before she came here. Maybe she was mistreated. She'll come around in time," her mother said. Across the room, Jasmine stared at her paws, feeling guilty. Why couldn't she love this little girl? She liked Elizabeth well enough, but she just felt too empty, too sad to love any other mirow.

After that day, Jasmine stopped sleeping on Elizabeth's bed, moving to the top shelf of the linen closet instead. Here she found the seclusion she yearned for.

Chapter Four

Every day Jasmine fell deeper into depression. She ate less and less. Her dreams were filled with Joel, so she slept as much as she could. When awake, she longed for him. She wondered why Bastet could ever have found her worthy of a blessing; she felt so weak and afraid.

She might have lived the rest of her life in this fashion until she faded out of existence. But one afternoon, curled up on her shelf in the linen closet, she fell into a dream that changed everything.

She found herself in the back seat of the car beside Joel, as she had been on countless trips to the cottage. The sight of him filled her with joy; with a strangled cry she put her front paws on his shoulder and nuzzled his cheek. But to her astonishment, Joel ignored her. He brushed absently at his face as though something had tickled him and continued talking to his parents who were in the front seat. When Jasmine cried out in her deep Siamese voice he didn't even turn his head. Then she understood that, although she could see him, Joel couldn't see her.

"No!" Joel said heatedly, "I don't want another cat!"

"I didn't want to upset you. When I saw the ad for the Siamese kittens I just thought you might like one. I know how much you miss Jasmine. Maybe a new kitten would help you get over losing her," Joel's mother told him.

"She's not lost. She's going to find her way back to me. If Jasmine was dead, I'd know." Joel scowled at the scenery speeding by. Jasmine gave a little cry of joy. He knew she was coming to him! He'd know if something had happened to her, just as she'd know if he was in trouble.

"Oh Joel, how can you believe Jasmine's still alive?" his mother cried.

"She is. I see her in dreams," Joel said, his voice breaking.

"All right. Let's change the subject," she sighed, "I don't want to spoil the day fighting. After we take the measurements for the new cottage we'll have a long look around the woods for any sign of her."

Joel laid his head back against the seat and put his walkman on, turning it up loud. Jasmine stretched across his lap and gazed up at him, her blue eyes swimming with adoration.

Her bliss suddenly turned into terror as the car was rocked by a tremendous impact. The screech of tearing metal filled her ears. She found herself tossed in a shrieking, tumbling hell. It seemed to go on forever, then it was simply gone. Jasmine was astonished to see, far below her, the twisted mess of a car, upside down. One tire, still intact, spun as if the car were nothing more than a child's overturned toy. She understood then that she had been in a terrible accident. In spite of that, she felt strangely calm. The shattered car continued to fall away from her and she realized she was rising. A warm sense of peace cradled her as she waited to see what would come next.

Then, with a sickening shock she realized Joel was still down there in the wreck. Her Joel.

"No!" she howled, her paws flailing as she fought to go back down. It was pointless. She continued to rise like a spark from a fire.

"Jasmine! Jasmine what are you doing here!" To her relief Joel was beside her, unhurt and finally able to see her. "What happened? Where are we?" Pale as wax, his eyes huge with shock, Joel stared at her. From far below came the wail of sirens, but they could no longer see the accident. They hung suspended in empty grey space; nothing above or below. It was impossible to tell if they were still rising.

Joel gathered the cat into his arms. "I don't know what's going on but I'm glad you're here." Jasmine squeezed her eyes shut, overwhelmed with happiness. By some miracle, they were together. But she felt a premonition that something was about to happen.

Far off, a bright speck appeared, slowly blossoming into a dazzling light. They felt themselves drawn closer to it, pulled like smoke to an open window.

"What is that?" Joel breathed. Dazed by the increasing brilliance, Jasmine narrowed her eyes.

Then, out of nowhere, a great dark shadow appeared before them, blocking out the light. "Go back!" a voice roared. The shadow swirled and took the form of a towering black cat. Gold rings hung from pointed ears and huge golden eyes pierced them like lasers. "It is not your time, or the boy's, to come to Summerland. Go back!" The voice was stern.

But I don't know how to go back, Jasmine thought, desperate. What do I do? She couldn't ask for help. This creature would annihilate her with a glance if she dared to speak. Surely this was Bastet, Queen of cats. Jasmine hadn't realized how terrifying she could be. She could feel Joel trembling. He too was afraid to speak. Jasmine looked beneath them at the grey nothingness.

"Down," she mewed in a shaky voice. Suddenly, she felt as if they were falling. "Down," she cried again and down they went in a slow spiralling descent like a dropped feather. Jasmine didn't dare to look back at the great cat.

"What's going on?" Joel cried as they fell. Burrowing beneath his chin Jasmine wondered as well. The light shrank to a pinprick and then disappeared altogether. She felt a sharp pang of sorrow leaving that brilliant place though she didn't know why.

Jasmine and Joel were tumbling faster now. Suddenly they were surrounded by green walls. Their fall stopped with a sickening lurch. A sharp smell of disinfectant pinched Jasmine's nose. She was no longer in Joel's arms; he was lying a narrow white bed, his distraught parents beside him. Jasmine found herself crouched on the bed as well, though Joel's parents didn't seem to see her. Joel looked like he was sleeping but Jasmine knew he wasn't. He had been away with her to the gates of Summerland, and now he was back. Jasmine could smell his parents' fear. She wished she could tell them not to be afraid, that Joel would soon wake.

With a whimper, Joel opened his eyes. They looked straight into Jasmine's and he smiled weakly.

"Jass, we're back," he whispered.

Everything went black.

Her own cries woke her. She found herself enclosed in a small dark space. She almost panicked until she saw light coming through a long vertical crack. Then Jasmine realized she was still on the shelf in the linen closet. Surely days had gone by since she had come here for a nap, but when she pushed open the door and jumped down she saw only a little time had passed. The same chicken was still roasting in the oven, and the light had changed only a little. Deeply shaken, she gave herself a calming wash as she thought about what had happened. This was no ordinary dream, she was certain. A sense of foreboding filled her. Joel had been in terrible danger. Was he safe now? Surely she would know if he wasn't, she told herself.

At that moment, Jasmine felt her heavy burden of despair begin to lighten. She belonged with Joel; the dream proved it. Their lives were so entwined nothing could keep them apart, not even death. Jasmine knew now that she couldn't live without trying to make it back to him.

She went to her dish and devoured the food, then took a long drink of water. She expected this would be her last good meal for a while. She wailed at the door until Elizabeth came from her room to let her out. Jasmine rubbed against Elizabeth, then stretched up on her back legs until the girl picked her up. Elizabeth buried her face in Jasmine's sweet-smelling coat.

"Nice kitty. Want to go out?" She gazed into Jasmine's blue eyes.

For the last time, the cat felt the pang of guilt. I hope Bastet sends you a cat of your own to love, she thought. It would be a very lucky cat. Jasmine gave the girl a tender feline kiss on the nose. With a giggle Elizabeth kissed Jasmine's velvety nose in return. Then she opened the door and let the cat out.

Jasmine jumped off the step, ran around the corner of the house and out of sight, her heart racing. She was glad to be out under the sky again. The outside world was indeed filled with danger but at that moment it seemed worth all the risks just to be free again.

By midnight, Truro was well behind her. The land rose somewhat as she left the saltmarshes behind. The moon was waxing towards full again and she felt exposed by its light. She continually checked for signs of coyotes that first night. Still, she was happy to be on the move. Jasmine felt strong again, stronger than ever. She was no longer the pampered, helpless cat who had begun the journey. Now she was a fierce huntress, a skillful provider. She had even conquered darkest despair.

By early morning she was tired and ready to rest. She made her bed halfway up a poplar tree. The narrow branches were uncomfortable but sleeping on the ground felt too risky.

Late in the afternoon she woke, rested and hungry. Climbing down, she nibbled some tender blades of grass, then hunted until dark, finally managing to catch and kill a fat deermouse. She ate it and, after a wash, went on her way.

Jasmine had turned slightly west since leaving Truro, pulled by her inner compass. She never questioned this instinctive urge; her faith had returned. With Bastet's help she would find Joel.

During the night a cold rain began to fall, soaking Jasmine as she travelled beneath the dripping trees. The moon's light was obscured behind banks of heavy cloud, but this made no difference to the cat. She could find her way through the darkest night.

When she came to a dense clump of spruce

trees she decided to shelter there until the rain stopped. Cautiously, she pushed her way through the thick branches. She climbed as far up into one bushy tree as she could and began to lick the wet from her fur. From beneath the tree rose the woodsy smell of wet ferns and the rich aroma of nearly-ripe wild raspberries. The wind lashed at the trees and flung curtains of rain at the spruce grove but in her prickly nest the cat was soon dry and comfortable.

As the night passed Jasmine realized she wasn't the only creature sheltering there. Faint flutters from above told her that birds were roosting in the higher branches. In the next tree something heavy shifted and murmured. At first Jasmine was alarmed but as the scent of the creature drifted over to her she relaxed. The smell was familiar. Though she couldn't quite identify it, it carried the harmless green aroma of an herbivore.

As the sky began to lighten, the wind dropped but the rain continued to patter down. The creatures in the spruce grove stirred restlessly but stayed put, unwilling to leave the shelter until hunger drove them out. The family of pine siskins roosting above Jasmine chirped a warning to one another as the growing light revealed the cat's presence. She paid no attention, knowing they were well out of her reach. In the next tree she could now see a bulky shape clinging to a thick branch. It was gnawing steadily at the bark, seemingly indifferent to everything around it.

Bored, Jasmine watched the slow-moving animal methodically strip away and devour the bark along the trunk, exposing the slick wet flesh beneath it. The creature's refusal to even acknowledge her existence began to irk Jasmine; small though she was, as a predator she expected a certain level of respect from a mere tree eater. Finally she called to it, "Hey, you there, what are you?"

The creature finished chewing its mouthful of bark before it raised its head and peered over at Jasmine. The face was blunt and round-eyed, its ears small. The body was stocky and covered with very bristly black hairs, and it had a heavy club-shaped tail.

"I am Cor the tree skinner. I hadn't noticed you there. Trying to keep dry are you hm-m-m?" His slow, stupid mumbling only annoyed Jasmine more.

"How could you not notice me? I've been right here all night!" she retorted.

Cor chewed meditatively at a strip of bark until it disappeared between his long front teeth.

"I'm a sound sleeper. Once I was asleep in a tree that blew down in the night and I didn't even wake up. There I was next morning buried under a heap of branches, wondering hm-m-m, what happened?"

Jasmine stared at him, hardly able to believe such a tale. What a stupid creature you must be, she thought. "Aren't you afraid of being attacked while you're sleeping so soundly?"

Reaching up with a long-clawed front foot, Cor began to inch his way up to the next branch. "Oh no, everyone around here pretty much leaves me alone." He chuckled to himself. "If they know what's good for them, hm-m-m-m. What are you by the way? I don't recall seeing anything like you before."

"My name is Jasmine. I am a Siamese cat," she replied with as much dignity as she could summon. Whether Cor heard she never knew; he resumed ripping bark and seemed to have lost interest in her. Offended, she turned her back to him and took a nap.

Rain fell through the long dreary day. Jasmine's stomach began sending such strong messages of hunger that she almost wished she could dine on the bark beneath her like the slow-witted Cor. Finally, in the early evening, the rain stopped, just as the setting sun cast watery beams of light through the dispersing clouds. When Jasmine woke from a cat-nap she saw that Cor had made his way to the ground.

Time for me to get moving too, she decided, stretching. She leapt lightly down. Though anxious to be on her way, she couldn't resist a closer look at Cor. "Goodbye, guess I'll be on my way," she told him.

"Hm-m-m, goodbye, little Siamese cat, have a safe night," he muttered, all the while eyeing the juicy fir tree next on his menu. Before Jasmine could think of a way to let him know how foolish she thought him, a nearby sound made her freeze in terror—the deep-throated baying of a dog. She flew back up into the spruce tree and crouched there, trembling. Branches snapped and a large, snarling shepherd burst into the spruce grove, his lips laid back to bare long white fangs. A length of broken chain dangled from his collar. He was lost, hungry and afraid. Ears back and tail down, he slunk towards Cor, a rumbling growl rising from him.

"Cor," Jasmine screamed, "get out of there! Climb up, quick!" But instead of fleeing, Cor turned his back to the dog and lashed his bristling tail. Jasmine looked away horrified, expecting to hear his death shriek, but to her amazement she heard the dog's howl of pain instead. Looking down she was astonished to see him backing away from Cor, a dozen of the sharp bristles lodged in his black muzzle. Raising his paw the dog rubbed them and squealed in pain. Every hair on Cor's body stood on end. Whimpering, the dog took one last look at him and crept away.

When she was certain the dog was not coming back Jasmine climbed down the tree and bowed her head respectfully to Cor. "There's more to you than meets the eye," she told him.

"I just want to be left alone, h-m-m-m. Most of the wild-born animals know that. The ones that don't find out the hard way."

"I—I guess," Jasmine said, thankful that she had not made that mistake. "Well goodbye again and good luck." She hurried away, suddenly mindful of how close she stood to his bristling tail.

The next few days and nights were uneventful. Prey was scarce again; mice that had survived the season were cautious and harder to catch. Once she found a late-season robin's nest and ate the new-laid eggs.

On the morning of the fourth day after her encounter with Cor she came to the banks of the broad, muddy Shubenacadie River. When

Jasmine came upon the river its bed was a wet, shining mudflat cut by a narrow channel of water. In the rosy light of the rising sun she saw flocks of semi-palmated sandpipers skittering along the water's edges, feeding on the tiny crustaceans left behind by the tide. Hunting took a turn for the better as she trotted through the mousey marsh grass. Grasshoppers sprang in every direction but Jasmine seldom had to resort to them.

The next few days of travel were the easiest she'd known as she followed the river inland. Everything under the hot mid-August sun seemed drowsy, from the drooping grasses to the slow-moving cattle in the fields. Every creature had food in abundance. Birds and animals feasted on the ripe bounty of blueberries, raspberries and Indian plums. Pollen-dusted bees droned high in stalks of goldenrod. Mice grew plump on the ripening grain.

Still sleeping through the hottest part of the day, Jasmine woke late each afternoon, hunted until she'd eaten her fill, then walked through the cool nights across marsh and meadow, following the river. There were fewer signs of predators as she came near farmland; owls were her main fear in such open spaces. Whenever she picked up a whiff of fox musk she longed for Yip and sent a quick plea to Bastet to watch over her little friend.

The river narrowed as she made her way into Shubenacadie one evening. Ahead, as far as she could see, were sweeping cornfields.

Suddenly a fresh, stiff breeze blew at her from the south-east and for the first time Jasmine caught a hint of the scent she'd been searching for, the cold salty breath of the Atlantic Ocean, many miles away. Though she had never seen that great body of water she knew her home was close to it. All her life she'd been reminded of the presence of the Atlantic Ocean every time a south wind blew through the open windows of Joel's house.

The corn towered high above her, blocking out the sun. It was impossible to see anywhere but straight ahead. At first this unnerved the cat but she soon became comfortable in the shelter the corn stalks provided. As night came, the faint light of the moon turned her path into a tunnel walled by rustling silvery leaves.

In the morning, tired and hungry, she stopped to hunt. There were few field mice in the corn fields so Jasmine had to make do with some spiky, unsatisfying grasshoppers. At the edge of a pasture she found a heap of brush-cut alders. She made an uncomfortable bed beneath them.

The shrill whine of cicadas woke her late in the afternoon. Although still weary, she squeezed out of the brush-pile, eager to be on the move again. While crossing the pasture, she caught the unlikely smell of fish. It took no time to locate the source, some ripe fish entrails lying in the long grass. Jasmine paused, puzzled to find such a thing in the middle of a field. In spite of the buzzing cloud of flies, it seemed edible, but there was a faint smell of something else beneath the reek of fish. Had she breathed deeper she would have picked up the bitter tang of metal under the bait, but hunger made her careless. She reached for the fish, putting her small brown paw directly on the bar that triggered the trap. Cruel metal jaws snapped shut.

The sudden shock made her spring back, causing a surge of agony. Cringing, she lay still, trying to understand what had happened. She saw that metal jaws had bitten deep just above her front foot. Blood trickled from the torn fur and shattered bones. Panting with fear, Jasmine tried to calm her pain and terror by staying very still.

The shadows lengthened as afternoon turned to evening and the little cat lay in a swoon. Deep in shock, she gradually became lost in a dream-world. She saw herself as a kitten chasing madly after a ball of foil, dropping it at Joel's feet so that he could throw it for her again and again. Then it was the time of year when the family brought a live tree into the house and draped it with shining balls that tinkled and shattered delightfully when batted about. This image faded and Jasmine saw Joel again. He was lying in the same bed he had been in after the accident. His face was pale, and his eyes closed. His mother sat beside him, talking in a soft voice, but Jasmine knew he didn't hear. His spirit, like hers, was lost, wandering somewhere. Sudden terror filled her as she stared at the motionless body in the hospital bed. Was this vision from the past, like the others, or was Joel in danger again?

A powerful voice began calling to her.

"Jasmine!"

She refused to listen. "Joel!" she cried.

The voice called again, closer now and insistent, and Jasmine's vision of Joel began to fade. Blackness blotted out the room. Two great golden eyes opened in the darkness and fixed Jasmine in their gaze.

"Bastet," Jasmine gasped, trembling.

"Be brave. I come to help you, little one." The black cat's voice was tender.

Jasmine's terror began to ease. "You can help me?" she asked, her voice faint.

The amber eyes blazed. "Of course. I have watched your long journey. Great love has kept you on this difficult path. I will not allow you to perish now."

"What about Joel? Is he all right?"

"I would not send you back if he was gone from your world."

Jasmine still felt uneasy. Did she mean Joel was out of danger? "Queen Bastet, I'm afraid to go back," she said. "There's so much pain."

"You must go back. You would not wish to remain here."

"No," Jasmine agreed.

"I will be with you. I have been with you all along. You are my child, as are all cats. So many suffer and die at the hands of mirows. I can do nothing but send them back to be born again. For you I am making an exception; I am giving you back your life. Look at me, Jasmine." The eyes of Bastet grew ever brighter and Jasmine felt their radiance warm her body and soul. "Close your eyes now," Bastet murmured. "Remember I am with you."

Shutting her eyes, Jasmine trembled with a fierce stab of pain. She was back in the field. A cry of despair rose in her throat. You said you would be with me, she cried silently, where are you?

Opening her eyes, she saw a pair of dusty boots and looked up to find a man standing over her. Her paw still throbbed fiercely but the open trap lay beside her in the grass. One of the boots prodded her gently in the ribs, provoking her to yowl a deep Siamese curse.

"You'll be all right then," the man muttered. He lifted her and tucked her under an arm as Jasmine once again faded from consciousness.

Chapter Five

Something sharp was poking her ear. Jasmine opened one eye to find herself lying on a bed of prickly straw. Pain still pulsed in her injured paw. Cautiously, she raised her head to find she was lying on the floor in a small wooden enclosure. Her nose told her she was not alone. The smell of grass-eating animals hung heavy in the air. High above, sunlight sifted through cracks in the weathered boards. New hay, still heavy with the sweet scent of clover and purple vetch, was stacked in the loft. Beside her she saw a pan of clean water. Gratefully, she leaned over and drank.

"Glad to see you're awake," a deep voice rumbled. Startled, Jasmine looked around but saw nothing except the dusty grey walls of her stall. She heard a bubbling snort and looked up, way up, to see a massive brown head peering down at her from the next stall. A blaze of white ran between his long ears to his velvety muzzle. He was the largest animal she had ever seen. She stared, unnerved. A grass-eater, by the smell of him. So at least he was unlikely to make a meal of her. The beast shook his great head and snorted again, fixing his long-lashed brown eyes on her.

"How are you feeling?" he asked in a kindly tone. "My name is Star. I'm a Percheron horse in case you were wondering."

Trembling, Jasmine decided it would be wise to try to befriend the monster. "My paw has been crushed," she replied timidly.

"I could tell you'd been hurt as soon as Max brought you in. Get some rest. It's the best thing for you right now. I'm sure you'll feel better soon." The wall between them shook as Star shifted himself back into his stall. Jasmine wondered what the rest of the creature looked like, given the size of his head. She gave her damaged paw a few tentative licks then, exhausted, fell into a long, deep sleep.

A rustling in the straw woke her early the next morning. She snapped to full alert, having no idea where she was. The man who had taken her from the trap knelt beside her. She suddenly remembered everything and cringed away.

"Here now, girl. It's okay. Eat something," he

murmured, placing a dish of soft cat food in front of her. In the shadows behind him Jasmine saw two tiger-striped cats lurking, their green eyes watching her every move. She feared the man but she was weak from hunger and the food smelled irresistible. Awkwardly, she stood on three shaking paws and began to eat. The man stayed near until she was done. To her relief, he made no attempt to touch her. After she finished eating he disappeared. As soon as he was out of sight the two grey cats approached. She saw at once they were not friendly. The fur on their backs bristled.

"This is our barn," hissed one of them, a thin, half-grown male, "and if you think we'll let you stay here, you're mistaken."

The older female spoke next. "If we find you hunting on our territory, we'll rip that mangey hide off your back."

Jasmine eyed them, shocked by their rudeness. Though all cats were territorial, there was an unspoken rule that a sick visitor should be left alone to heal. Surely the huge barn and wide fields beyond could hold all of them.

Suddenly the floor beneath her shook and she looked up to see her giant neighbour again.

"You leave her alone, Grey Cat. She's too sick

to be any trouble to you." The cats glared up at him, their ears laid back against their skulls, neither of them moving. "Go on then, both of you!" Star gave a stamp that made Jasmine's teeth rattle. With a parting hiss the two cats fled.

"Thank you. I was hoping to avoid a fight," she told him, grateful for his intervention. "I haven't properly introduced myself. My name is Jasmine."

"Don't worry about those two, Jasmine. They're bullies. Once you're well enough to fight back they'll leave you alone."

"Can you tell me where I am?" she asked. "I don't remember anything after that mirow took those biting jaws from my paw."

"Certainly. You're at Marshbrook farm. Max, the man who just fed you, is the human who takes care of us. I guess you cats would call him our mirow. Mostly cattle live here, a few chickens, and me, the last heavy horse on the place." He tossed his head proudly.

"I've never seen anything like you," Jasmine said, guessing that he wanted her to understand he was no ordinary farm animal.

"There aren't a lot of us left. Most of the farmers around here can't afford a valuable beast like me. They have to make do with noisy, unreliable machines instead, tractors and such. But where do you come from, if you don't mind me asking?"

Jasmine told Star everything that had happened to her since the fire in the cottage.

"You've been through a lot for such a little creature," he said when she finished her story. "What will you do now?"

She looked at her paw, the torn skin just beginning to heal over the exposed bone. "I'm not too far from home, maybe a few weeks, but . . . my paw. I don't know if I'll ever be able to walk on it again. I don't know how I'll have the strength to finish my journey." Overcome by grief, she lay down in the straw and shut her eyes. To be this close and never get to Joel. It was more than she could bear.

A velvety soft muzzle brushed across her face and when Jasmine opened her eyes she was looking directly into Star's. His tangled forelock hung across his gentle dark eyes and his moist breath tickled her whiskers.

"Don't give up, Jasmine. You'll find a way to get home. You'll see." Hearing Star's words, Jasmine remembered what Bastet had told her: I will be with you. Who was she, Jasmine, to doubt the promise of the Queen of Cats?

Jasmine gave Star's long muzzle a lick with her rough pink tongue. "Thank you. Your heart is as big as the rest of you," she told him. "You're right, I won't give up now."

He gave a low whinny in a blast of sweet-smelling, grassy breath. "Brave cat. Good for you."

"Star, do you know anything about the metal thing that bit my paw?"

"It was a trap put out for racoons; they love ripe corn." Star hesitated a moment. "Max puts down the traps to catch them."

Jasmine stared up at him, astonished. "M a x put that terrible thing there? How could he?"

Star's dark eyes were troubled. "Who can understand why humans act as they do? I don't know why they like some creatures while they kill others on sight. But I'm certain Max didn't mean to hurt you, Jasmine. He's been doing his best to help you get better."

Licking her ruined paw, Jasmine reflected upon the strangeness of mirows. At least Joel would never cause such hurt to another creature. She was sure of that.

While Jasmine rested at Marshbrook, the blue and gold days of August passed. Star was free to go to the paddock outside, but when he was in, he and the cat passed the long hours in comfortable companionship. The unlikely pair quickly became close friends. He cheered her on as she tried to regain her agility but she began to realize she would never be able to walk on her damaged front paw. The shattered bones knit together but they were hopelessly crushed.

Every afternoon, Jasmine practised leaping to the top of the wall between their stalls. It was a big jump, even for a cat with four good paws, but she was determined to do it. She knew she would feel safer if she could get off the stall floor. Time after time, she leaped and dug into the wooden wall with the claws of her good front paw, her strong back legs kicking furiously as she tried to push herself up. But every attempt ended with a tumble into the straw.

"Try again," Star urged when she found herself yet again shaking straw from her ears. Sometimes Jasmine would stalk off in disgust at this point, but more often, she would try one more jump.

When she finally did make it to the top of the wall she clung to it for dear life, her tail switching with excitement. From her new height she could see all around the barn. Star tossed his head in excitement.

"I knew you'd get here! Every day you've been getting closer."

Jasmine rubbed her chin against the wood possesively. "I can't believe I did it! I love it up here!" She stretched along the wall, purring with satisfaction.

On warm days, Jasmine began leaving the barn to explore outside though she never strayed far. Max's white farm house sat near the old barn on the top of a rolling hill. To the south stretched corn fields. To the west were pastures, dotted with slow-moving black and white Holstein cattle. The dairy cattle had their own barn, a big shining steel structure nothing like the weathered old barn that housed Star, the cats and a few fussy old hens.

On a rainy day two weeks after her arrival, Jasmine had her next run-in with the two barn cats. That day, instead of giving Jasmine her usual dish of food, Max picked her up and carried her across the barn where the other cats were fed.

"You've been spoiled long enough," he told her. From a nearby feed bin he scooped dry kibble into a big metal bowl. "Time for you to dine with the other cats. They won't mind sharing with you."

Jasmine answered him with an anxious yowl. She was sure the two barn cats would mind very much. She could see them in the loft above, glaring down at her. As soon as Max left, they sprang down like two furies.

"Get back! This is ours!" they growled in unison. Jasmine crouched by the dish and faced them, disgusted by their greed. The hair on her back rose in a sharp ridge, her ears flattened against her skull, and her tail grew as big as a bottle brush. Baring her fangs, she spat at the two cats, making them pause to take her measure. For a small, lame cat she suddenly looked very fierce. Tail lashing, she fixed her blue eyes on them and stared them down.

"Back off! There's plenty of food here for all of us!" she warned in her deepest Siamese snarl. The young male backed quickly away but the female, Grey Cat, held her ground.

"Get away from our food and out of our barn!" she yowled.

"I'll stay here as long as I please," Jasmine replied, relishing the thought of digging her claws into Grey Cat's hide. In her rage, she forgot all about her crippled paw. For several long minutes the two cats glared at one another, ears back, tails switching.

Jasmine could see her unexpected ferocity surprised the other cat. Her dark masked face and blue eyes seemed to unnerve Grey Cat as well. To Jasmine's great satisfaction, the barn cat soon backed off and slunk out of the barn, trailed by her companion.

Though the excitement of the encounter had taken away most of her appetite Jasmine ate what she could from the communal dish, then returned to her stall. Only when she was back in her own space and feeling secure did Jasmine realize what she had done; she had squared off against two fierce barn cats and won. Even the terrible ordeal in the trap had not destroyed her. So I only have three paws—I can take care of myself just fine, she told herself. She crossed the barn to her stall with new confidence, head and tail held high.

The nights grew cold as August gave way to September. Jasmine burrowed into the straw after dark and still lay awake shivering.

"I'm freezing. When does the heat get turned on?" she asked Star one morning after an uncomfortable night.

He whickered in amusement. "There is no heat in here, except from our bodies. It's going to get a lot colder than this, too. Don't you know about winter?" he asked.

Jasmine leapt clumsily to the top of the wall between their stalls and began to lick the chill from her fur. "Sure, but I've never been out in it, I've lived in a house all my life," she reminded him, smoothing a cream-coloured flank. "What will I do, Star? My fur isn't thick enough for winter cold."

Star tossed his head, considering. "Can you jump from the wall to my back? You'd be warm and I wouldn't even notice you—you don't weigh much more than a dandelion seed."

Jasmine looked at the horse's broad brown back. "You wouldn't mind? Really?" The cat studied the gap between them, considering. "Hold still then, get ready . . ." Jasmine made an uncertain leap from the wall to the horse, scrambling to keep from slipping to the floor far below.

"Hey! Watch those claws!" Star complained, shifting slightly.

"Sorry. Sorry. I'll get better at this, I promise," Jasmine told him, stretching out along Star's back. "O-o-oh, this is much better. You're as good as a furnace."

"Why are you still shivering then?"

Jasmine nuzzled against Star's tangled mane. "I'm not, I'm purring."

When Max came into the barn a short while later he took one look at the cat perched tidily on his horse's back and laughed.

"Found yourself a warm place for the winter, I see. Aren't you a clever cat?"

The next day was bright and warm, for autumn. Star woke Jasmine from a nap. "Better jump down, I'm going outside for a while," he told her.

The cat peered out through the barn door at the paddock. The thought of lying in the sun appealed to her, too. But leaping down off the big horse wasn't easy. If she jarred her injured paw when she landed it ached for hours. "Go ahead, I'm staying up here."

Star huffed uncertainly, his great sides heaving.

"I'm getting better at balancing," Jasmine coaxed, "I haven't fallen off yet and I hardly ever have to use my claws to hang on."

"Oh, all right. You can't be worse than some of the humans who've sat on me," he grumbled, and he moved out of the barn so carefully that each huge hoof might have been made of china. Jasmine sprawled out, hugging tight to the contours of his back. It was easier than she'd expected. In a moment they were in the meadow, the cat still aboard. She drank in the sun's heat while Star pulled at ragged tufts of grass with his strong teeth.

The autumn afternoon was glorious. In the distance, cattle foraged on sparse grass remaining in the pasture. A few late butterflies danced dizzily among clumps of aster and goldenrod along the fence line. Robins ransacked a nearby mountain ash tree, filling up on the scarlet berries. Gazing up into the cerulean blue sky, Jasmine felt a sense of peace she hadn't known since before the fire. She was sure she could feel the power and protection of Bastet in the sun's heat and she was more than content to bask in it, as all cats are.

The first frost came soon after. When Jasmine left the barn just after sunrise, she saw the white skim of ice crystals melting away into the grass. She could smell the decay of foliage that had grown so vigorously through the summer. Later that day Max appeared, his arms filled with leather and brass harnesses. Seeing them, Star whinnied with excitement.

"You remember, don't you big fella," Max smiled, rubbing the horse's neck. Jasmine settled on top of the wall between their stalls, curious to see what would happen next.

Untangling the shining straps, Max began to fasten them across Star's chest and head and flanks. Star didn't object to this. He stamped and tossed his head eagerly while Max worked. Finally Max led the horse out of the barn, across the paddock, and out of sight. Jasmine ventured out and looked around, nagged by worry. Where had they gone? Max had never taken Star away before. Then she saw a great wooden box on wheels in the driveway beside the house. Another horse just like Star was tied to the front of it. As she watched, Max placed Star beside this horse and fastened him to the wheeled box. Then Max climbed up onto the box and gave the lines that bound the horses a shake. They trotted briskly down the driveway until Max gave a shout and tugged on the lines. Then the horses turned together and pulled him in another direction. They repeated the same moves over and over until Jasmine finally grew bored and returned to her stall for a nap.

An hour later Max brought Star back to the barn. He shook a half-pail of oats into the horse's trough. While Star ate, snorting and blowing, Max curried his coat until it gleamed. Paws folded beneath her, Jasmine lay on the top of the wall and watched, blinking sleepily. When Max was finished he hung up the brush, paused to scratch Jasmine under her chin, then left.

"What were you and Max doing, and who was that other horse?" she asked, puzzled.

His eyes bright with anticipation, Star said "Fair time is coming. That's when we go away and stay in a huge barn filled with animals and people. Prince, the horse you saw today, goes with us; we have the same sire so we make a good matched pair. Prince lives just down the road and his human lets Max take him at fair time. We get to pull a wagon around in the big dirt paddock for Max while all the people watch. It's great fun!"

"It is? I don't think I'd like it at all. Don't all those people get on your nerves?" she asked.

"Well sometimes, but it's worth it. There's so much excitement, so much going on. And I get to see horse friends I'd never see otherwise." Star suddenly raised his head and stared at Jasmine, wide-eyed. "I just had a great idea. Why don't you come with me this year?"

"I don't know. I'd be afraid I'd get stepped on, what with people and horses tramping everywhere," Jasmine told him.

"Oh come on, it's only a couple of days. I'll look out for you. It would be a great adventure." Star switched his tail impatiently. "At least think about it."

Jasmine jumped lightly onto his back and began to wash her face. "I will," she promised.

During the next couple of weeks Max spent all his spare time working with Star and Prince. Jasmine watched from a safe distance, admiring their shining brown coats and the harnesses with the brass medallions that twinkled in the autumn sunlight. Max spent evenings currying and brushing Star until even the long white hair over his great hoofs shone.

Jasmine might never have gone with him if the two barn cats had left her alone. She spent her afternoons in the loft stalking mice to keep in practice while Star went through his paces with Prince. Jasmine knew she wouldn't be able to continue her journey until spring. Travelling would be hard enough now with her injury; the winter weather would be more than she could cope with. As she crouched in the hay one afternoon, searching for a whiff of rodent, the two cats came slinking towards her. Grey Cat stared insolently, her green eyes full of spite. Finally, she spoke. "We hear that Star invited you to go to the fair with him."

"And what business is it of yours?" Jasmine asked calmly.

"Tell him you're not going, if you know what's good for you. You don't belong here, and we don't want anyone thinking you do."

"I'd like to see you stop me," Jasmine growled. The hair rose on the backs of the other cats.

"We'll claw you to shreds!" the male cat snarled.

"You don't scare me, little kitten," Jasmine told him.

"Listen, you stupid cat," the female broke in, "you've been warned. Our good reputation isn't going to be ruined by a scrawny, ugly cripple like you."

Jasmine looked at them. Their grey fur was matted and dirty. The male cat was missing half an ear. Grey Cat's eyes were oozing pus from a chronic infection. "Have you had a look at yourselves lately?" she asked. "Didn't your mother ever teach you to wash?"

The male cat spat at her. Baring her white fangs, Jasmine sent him scurrying with a single hiss. Grey Cat herself held her ground, facing off against Jasmine for several long minutes. She howled with rage and Jasmine answered with a high, sing-song wail of her own.

Then, the sound of Star's heavy step grew near as Max led him back to his stall. Grey Cat snarled and ran off. Jasmine leapt to the dividing wall between her stall and Star's and watched Max curry the big horse.

As soon as he hung up the brush and left, Jasmine announced, "I've decided to take you up on your offer to go to the fair."

Chapter Six

"Come as close as you can. Then, when no one's looking, slip in," Star advised as they watched from the barn. A truck towing a high, narrow silver box had backed up nearby.

"Is that what we're riding in?" Jasmine asked, staring at it. They could hear Prince whinnying anxiously inside.

"Sure. It's a horse trailer. I've been in it lots of times. Prince is always a little nervous at first, but he'll settle down once we're on the road. There's nothing to be afraid of."

They could see Max coming for Star. "Stay away from Prince's feet when you get in," he warned.

"Don't worry, I'm not planning to be stomped flat before I even leave the yard," Jasmine assured him. But watching Max lead Star into the trailer she was filled with misgivings. How would she manage to get in unnoticed?

More importantly, how could she avoid being stepped on? While Max was busy tying Star's halter to the front of the trailer, Jasmine knew the moment had come. She limped across the paddock, under the fence, and up the ramp, slipping into the shadows beneath Star's big feet. Sensing her presence, Star held himself as still as a statue.

"Good fella. You're not worried are you?" Max crooned, stroking Star's neck. Jasmine huddled motionless in the straw, unnoticed by the man. He swung the door shut and bolted it. The truck rumbled to life and the trailer began to sway. Star shifted to keep his balance. A sharp feline curse rang out at his feet.

"Bastet's whiskers! Be careful. You nearly stepped on me!"

"Sorry—I couldn't help it. Climb onto my back. You'll be safer there."

"I can't. There's not enough room to jump and the walls are too smooth to climb. Why didn't we think of this before? I'm trapped down here under your big clumsy feet," she wailed.

"Calm down. I've got a plan. I'm going to kneel and you can try to climb onto my back. Ready?"

"I don't know. Be careful!" Jasmine mewed.

"I won't hurt you." Bending his front legs, Star lowered himself slowly and awkwardly in the small space. Jasmine squeezed from beneath him and sprang onto his shoulders. Sprawling across him for balance, she held on as tightly as she dared while he stumbled to his feet.

"What's going on over there? What are you doing?" Prince whinnied, his voice shrill with fear.

"Nothing." Star told him. "I'm just getting Jasmine up off the floor."

"Hey, glad you decided to come along with us, Jasmine," Prince said, sounding a little calmer. "Star's always talking about you. You'll have a great time once we get out of this horrible shaking box."

The next few hours passed uneventfully. Jasmine and Star dozed fitfully in the rocking trailer while Prince shuffled restlessly on his short lead. Late that morning, Jasmine wokc from a dream. Like all her dreams of Joel, it was bitter-sweet; so real until the waking. But this dream seemed more real than any. In it, Joel was sleeping and she was curled up beside him, her head beneath his chin, blissfully happy, until the trailer gave a sudden lurch and woke her. Instead of feeling sad, as she usually did after such dreams, Jasmine felt strangely contented, as if she was still with her beloved mirow.

From her perch on Star's back the cat saw the

landscape pass in a blur through the narrow, dirty windows of the horse trailer. Even though she saw only glimpses of fields and rocky forests they looked oddly familiar. She had been travelling too long, she decided. Everything was beginning to look the same.

Around midday, the truck slowed and came to a creaking halt. Through the window, Jasmine could see a parking lot with a huge barn-like building nearby.

Star tossed his head eagerly. "We're here Jasmine. Can't you smell it! You're going be so glad you came!"

Giving one of his brown ears a lick, Jasmine replied, "I hope I like it half as much as you do."

Max swung open the trailer doors a few minutes later to find his Siamese barn cat curled up on Star's back.

"I see there's no separating you two," he smiled, "come on then, out you go." By the time Star was backed out and into his new stall, a small crowd had gathered around. Mostly horse people.

"Quite the hood ornament your horse has there," joked one man. Max grinned and said nothing. From her vantage point Jasmine tried to take in her new surroundings. The hard concrete floors made the horses' hooves ring out as they were led to and fro. The building seemed vast, long rows of stalls with metal barred doors running the length of it. High above, rows of fluorescent lights cast a cold glare. The smell of disinfectant and hay and oats hung in the air, but the earthy, sweet smell of horses and cattle was stronger. Max settled Prince into the stall beside Star, filled their mangers with hay, then went off to park the truck and trailer.

As the afternoon wore on, more and more people wandered through the barns. Some led horses, others were there to look at the animals. Jasmine stayed on Star's back, well out of the way of trampling feet. The sense of peace her dream had brought clung to her all day. She was glad she had decided to come to the fair but, watching the passing crowds, she was thankful to be beyond their reach. Many people stopped to point and stare at her and Star. Children, especially boys, caught her attention. Some of the boys were loud and wild, some quiet. Jasmine studied every one of them. They were nothing like Joel, she decided. No one was. She began to wash, trying to get him off her mind for a while.

Late in the afternoon Max returned with a bag of cat chow and a bowl of water for Jasmine. With him was a young woman carrying an odd-looking machine. Perking her ears, Jasmine watched uneasily as the woman raised the machine to her face. A faint whirring came from it. Beneath Jasmine, Star continued to doze, unconcerned. After a moment, the woman lowered the machine and she and Max chatted, just beyond earshot. When she left Max returned to the stall, looking pleased.

"Guess what?" he said, rubbing Star's nose. "You and your little friend here are going to be on the front page of the morning paper tomorrow. Not bad, huh?"

Gently he set Jasmine down in the straw and gave her the kibble and water, then he returned to the never-ending task of grooming the two horses.

Jasmine stretched her legs within the narrow confines of the stall. She had no idea of what Max was talking about. She didn't need to be on any papers; the straw made a fine litter box.

Early the next morning, Max led the horses out of the stalls and Jasmine was left alone. For a little while she slept in the hay in Star's manger but the rising noise soon woke her.

She saw a ledge where the metal bars of the stall met the wooden walls. After two misses, she managed to jump onto it. From there she could see everything while staying comfortably out of reach. Not far away, she could hear clapping, loud music and voices; she wondered if it was the great dirt paddock Star had described, where flocks of humans came to admire the skill of the horses. Although she wished she could see Star perform, she found the crowds of people and animals overwhelming. She had no intention of leaving the safe confines of Star's stall.

Several people passed leading dogs. Jasmine glared down at them uneasily. But the dogs appeared to be well-behaved, because crowds of children gathered to pet them. With distaste, she watched as some of the dogs allowed the pads of their paws to be painted, then pressed on papers that were then given to the children.

"Hey cat, want my autograph?" one impudent dog called. Glancing down Jasmine saw a shaggy black and white creature quivering with excitement.

"No, thank you," she replied haughtily.

"Suit yourself. It's your loss—we Superdogs are the stars of the show here you know."

"Oh—and what about the horses?" she retorted. Really, she thought, he was too conceited for words and had a most unsettling stare. Taking another look, she realized he had one blue eye and one brown one.

"Horses—hah!" he yipped, "Can a horse race

through a tunnel or retrieve a baton? Can a horse climb a ladder?"

Uncertain whether a horse could, in fact, do any of these things, Jasmine decided to change the subject. "What's your name?" she asked.

"I'm Jack, the smartest Border collie in Halifax."

"Halifax? You're from Halifax? How far is it from here?" she cried, scrambling to her feet.

At that moment, Jack's owner gave a tug on his lead and began to pull him away. Just before he disappeared into a sea of legs he called out, "Silly cat! Don't you even know where you are? This IS Halifax!"

Stunned, Jasmine tried to digest the news. How could it be? After all she had gone through, she was actually here at last and she hadn't even known it. Why hadn't it occured to her that the fair might be in Halifax? Now she knew why Joel had been on her mind so much since she'd left the farm.

By the time Star and Prince returned to their stalls she was beside herself with excitement. She jumped from the wall to the horse's back without sheathing her claws.

"Yow! Careful!" Star whinnied.

"Why didn't you tell me this fair is IN HAL-IFAX!" Jasmine cried.

"It is? I didn't know!"

"You ninny! Don't you get it? I'm here. Finally. All I have to do is figure out how to find my home." Jasmine glanced around the enormous barn. "But Halifax is huge. I don't even know how to get out of this building. What should I do, Star?"

"Take it easy. I know how anxious you must be but we'll be here for a couple of days. You don't have to go rushing off right now. We'll ask around and try to get some directions."

"I don't think I can stand to wait," Jasmine wailed.

"You can't go running off, you'll be stepped on or run over. Why don't you give yourself a good wash? You always say it relaxes you," Star suggested.

"You're so sensible and wise, you should have been a cat." Jasmine rubbed her masked face affectionately against the horse's shoulder, then gave herself a rather distracted cat-bath.

When evening came, the crowds at last began to thin. Star did his best to keep Jasmine calm as they discussed her next move. It had been a long day for both of them. When Max returned, Jasmine paid no mind, at first. Though she couldn't see him, she could hear Max talking to another man. After a moment, something about the man's voice caught her ear. She knew that voice. Springing to her feet, Jasmine peered through the bars of the stall. A woman and a pale boy, supported by two sticks, were coming toward her. For a second, Jasmine's heart stopped beating. It was Joel.

In the same instant, he cried, "It's her! It's Jasmine!"

She gave a strangled cry. The boy let his crutches fall with a clatter and grabbed the door of the stall.

Max laid his hand on Joel's shoulder. "Hello, I'm Max. This your cat?" he asked with a grin.

"Y—yes," the boy stammered.

Max swung the heavy bolt and opened the stall door. Reaching in, he scooped Jasmine off Star's back, and placed her in Joel's arms. Leaning against the wall for balance, Joel buried his face in Jasmine's soft, creamy fur. Purrs vibrated through her little body.

Finally he raised his face and looked at her. "Dad, her paw. She's hurt."

"We'll bring her to a vet tomorrow. She's been through a lot," Joel's father said, his voice sounding strangely husky. "When I phoned the paper, the reporter gave me Max's name. I came down here right away; the cat in that picture looked so much like Jasmine. She was asleep when I got here and I couldn't find Max. I didn't like to go into the stall beside that big horse on my own but I was pretty much certain she was Jasmine."

He turned to Max. "Joel's still recovering from a bad car accident. He's missed his cat so much. I don't know how to thank you for saving her."

"Saving her?" Joel asked. Max told him the story, starting with his discovery of the cat in a leg-hold trap. Joel held her tightly as Max described finding her, nearly dead.

Joel looked into Jasmine's blue eyes. "I always knew she was alive," he said quietly. He laid his face next to hers. "You brought me back to life," he said, in a voice only Jasmine could hear.

Joel's mother put her arm around him. "It's true, you never lost faith in her, not for a minute. This . . . miracle is a little overwhelming. I guess we'll never know the whole story. Joel, we'd better get you home, you shouldn't be on your feet this long."

Jasmine gave a sudden twist and leapt from Joel's arms. She ran back into Star's stall. "Goodbye, Star," she mewed. "You've been such a good friend. I'd never have gotten here if not for you. I'll miss you!"

The big horse lowered his head until he and

the cat were nose to nose. "I'll miss you too, little cat. Marshbrook won't be the same without you."

Jasmine gave him a cat kiss while the humans watched with puzzled smiles. Max seemed to understand. He gave Star a rub on the neck.

"You're gonna be lost without her, aren't you fella?"

The cat returned to Joel and yowled. Joel's dad scooped her up and placed Jasmine in Joel's arms, then handed him a crutch to lean on. Fixing her blue eyes on her mirow's beloved face, Jasmine quickly thanked Bastet, Queen of cats, whose promises were never broken.

A smile lit Joel's wan face. "Let's go home, Jasmine."

A NOTE ABOUT *JASMINE'S JOURNEY*

Jasmine's Journey begins at a cottage on the Amherst Shore, in northern Nova Scotia. Here, the Northumberland Strait divides Nova Scotia and Prince Edward Island. The warm water and sandbars make this a popular beach area. Jasmine follows this coastline until she crosses the Shinimicas River, then she ventures slightly to the south to enter the pretty little town of Pugwash.

After her adventures there, she continues south, crossing the neck of the province, also known as the Isthmus of Chignecto. She meets Yip in the dense forests covering the Wentworth hills. Crossing Wentworth in a south-easterly direction Jasmine eventually reaches Cobequid Bay. Here, she is forced to turn east, to the fields and marshland surrounding Truro.

When Jasmine leaves her temporary home in Truro's outskirts she again heads south, drawn to the distant Atlantic Ocean. There are more fields to cross; more forests. As she nears the gently rolling hills of Shubenacadie she finds farms and corn fields. Jasmine follows the Shubenacadie river as it meanders down from Cobequid Bay. Marshbrook farm is in this area, just beyond the river.

From Marshbrook, Jasmine's journey continues south to the Atlantic Winter Fair, which is held every October in Halifax, Nova Scotia's capital city.